O9-BTJ-589

DATE DUE

MAY 2 0 2008			

With gratitude to the original pea pals:
Andy, Tyler, Lincoln, Boone, Jacqueline, and Renee.

And to the little girl who asked me to please make up a naptime story,
this book is dedicated to you, Paris Anne. —A. K. R.

To Margaret Esther. —J. C.

Text © 2005 by Amy Krouse Rosenthal.
Illustrations © 2005 by Jen Corace.
All rights reserved.

Book design by Kristine Brogno.
Typeset in Messcara.
The illustrations in this book
were rendered in ink and watercolor.
Manufactured in China.

Library of Congress Cataloging-in-Publication Data
Rosenthal, Amy Krouse.
Little Pea / by Amy Krouse Rosenthal ;
illustrated by Jen Corace.
p. cm.
Summary: Little Pea hates eating candy for dinner,
but his parents will not let him have his spinach
dessert until he cleans his plate.
ISBN-13: 978-0-8118-4658-5
ISBN-10: 0-8118-4658-X
[1. Peas—Fiction. 2. Food habits—Fiction.]
I. Corace, Jen, ill. II.
Title.
PZ7.R719445Li 2005
[E]—dc22
2004013364

10 9 8 7

Chronicle Books LLC
680 Second Street
San Francisco, California 94107

www.chroniclekids.com

Little Pea

By Amy Krouse Rosenthal • Illustrated by Jen Corace

chronicle books · san francisco

This is the story of
Little Pea, Mama Pea, and Papa Pea.

Little Pea was a happy little guy.

He liked to do a lot of things.

He liked rolling down hills, for example,

super fast.

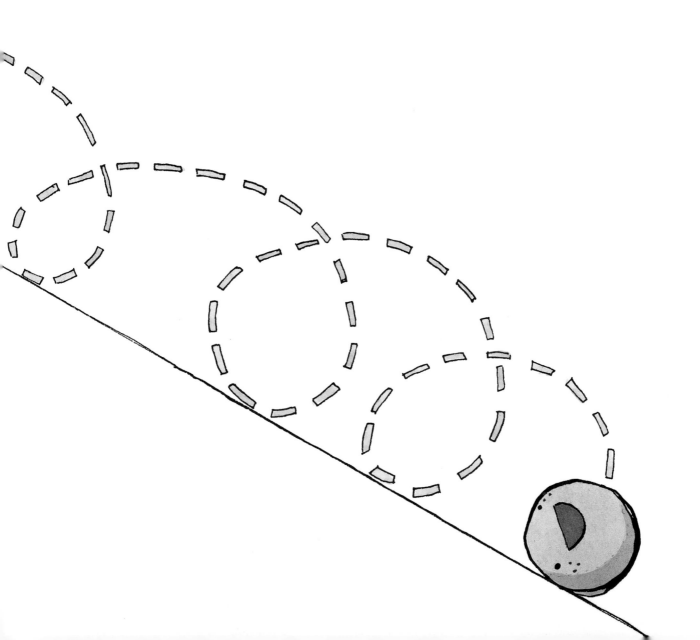

He liked hanging out with his pea pals.

He liked it when Papa Pea came home at the end of the day.
Papa Pea would fling Little Pea off a spoon
high into the air, and Little Pea would scream,
"Again! Again!"

At bedtime Little Pea very much liked snuggling with Mama Pea, and hearing stories about what Mama Pea was like when she was a little pea.

But there was one thing
that Little Pea did not like ...

Candy.

That's what you have to eat for dinner
every night when you're a pea.
Candy. Candy. Candy.

Monday:

Red Candy.

Tuesday:
Orange candy.

Thursday:

Purple and pink
polka-dotted candy.

Wednesday:
Yellow candy.

Friday:
Striped candy.

Saturday:
Swirly candy.

Sunday:
Rainbow candy.

Little Pea hated all of it.

"If you want to grow up to be a big, strong pea, you have to eat your candy," Papa Pea would say.

"If you don't finish your candy then you can't have dessert," Mama Pea would say.

"How many pieces do I have to eat?"

"Eat five pieces and you can have dessert."

"Five pieces?" he whined.

"Five pieces," they chimed.

"One. Yuck."

"Two. Blech."

"Three. Plck."

"Four. Pleh."

"Five pieces of candy! Now can I have dessert?"

"Yes. Now you can have dessert,"
said Mama Pea and Papa Pea.

Little Pea couldn't wait to see what it was.

"Spinach!"

squealed Little Pea.

"My favorite!"

Little Pea licked his dessert plate clean.

yum   yum   extra yum

FIG. 1   FIG. 2   FIG. 3

And they lived hap-pea-ly ever after.

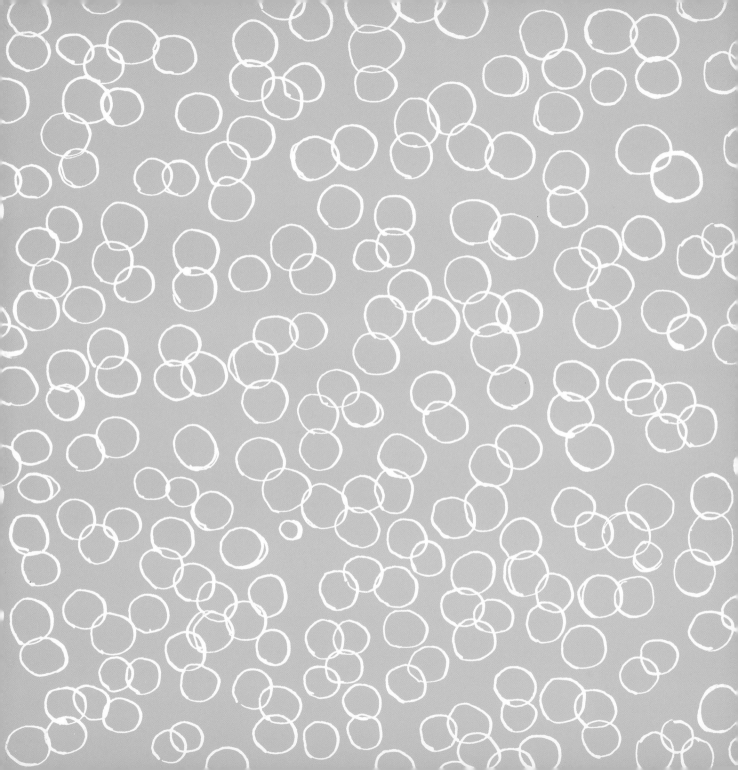